Vincent A. Smith

Remains Near Kasia in the Gorakhpur District

Vincent A. Smith

Remains Near Kasia in the Gorakhpur District

ISBN/EAN: 9783337386962

Printed in Europe, USA, Canada, Australia, Japan

Cover: Foto ©Andreas Hilbeck / pixelio.de

More available books at **www.hansebooks.com**

THE REMAINS NEAR KASIA,

IN THE

GŌRAKHPUR DISTRICT,

THE REPUTED SITE OF KUÇANAGARA OR KUÇINÂRA. THE SCENE OF
BUDDHA'S DEATH.

By VINCENT A. SMITH, I.C.S.,

Fellow of the University of Allahabad.

ALLAHABAD:

PRINTED AT THE NORTH-WESTERN PROVINCES AND OUDH GOVERNMENT PRESS.

1 8 9 6.

Price Rs.- 1-8-0.

CONTENTS.

——o——

PREFATORY NOTE.

—:◦◦:—

THE following Memorandum on the Buddhist remains near Kasiá has been prepared at the desire of Sir Antony MacDonnell, Lieutenant-Governor of the North-Western Provinces, who requested me to visit Kasiá, and submit proposals for the conservation of the monuments existing there. In accordance with His Honor's wishes I devoted three days at the end of January, 1896, to a minute examination of the Buddhist remains near Kasiá and of the surrounding country. When I went out there I shared the belief so confidently expressed by the late Sir Alexander Cunningham that the remains near Kasiá represent the ancient Kuçanagara, where the founder of the Buddhist religion died. Study of the local facts quickly convinced me that the site of Kuçanagara is not at or near Kasiá.

The true site yet remains to be discovered. Although it is at present beyond my power to determine precisely the site of Kuçanagara, I venture to think that the following pages conclusively demonstrate the negative proposition that the remains near Kasiá have no concern with the famous little town where the great master passed away, and the " Eye of the world " closed in death. The failure to establish a positive conclusion is to be regretted, but the destruction of error is the first step towards the attainment of truth; and the discovery of the true site of Kuçanagara will be made easier by the refutation of the erroneous theory which has been generally accepted for many years.

V. A. S.

THE REMAINS NEAR KASIĀ,

IN THE

GŌRAKHPUB DISTRICT,

THE REPUTED SITE OF KUÇANAGARA OR KUÇINĀRĀ, THE SCENE OF BUDDHA'S DEATH.

¶.—INTRODUCTORY.

THE identification of Kasiā with Kuçanagara, or Kuçinārā[1], the scene of the death of the founder of the Buddhist religion, has been generally considered for many years past to be an established fact. When Sir Antony MacDonnell recently asked me if I considered the identification certain, I felt no hesitation in replying that I believed it to be correct, and when I went out to Kasiā at the end of January 1896, to arrange for the conservation of the interesting remains there, I fully believed that the question as to the identity of Kasiā and Kuçanagara had been set at rest by the excavations and investigations of Sir Alexander Cunningham and his assistant Mr. A. C. Carlleyle.

Much to my surprise and dissatisfaction, a study of the remains on the spot has convinced me that Kasiā cannot possibly be the site of Kuçanagara, or Kuçinārā, and that the identification which has been generally accepted as established truth, is largely based upon misstatements of fact and fallacious reasoning. Since my visit to Kasiā I have learned that Dr. Waddell, the well-known authority on Lamaist Buddhism, independently arrived several years ago at the conclusion that Cunningham's identification of Kasiā with Kuçanagara cannot be supported[2].

Before entering on the controversy as to identification it will be convenient first to describe accurately the remains near Kasiā as they now exist, and secondly to describe the ancient city of Kuçanagara, or Kuçinārā, so far as the available documents permit. I propose to conclude my observations by recommendations for the conservation and further excavation of the extant remains, which, though not on the site of Kuçanagara,

[1] Kasiā, the headquarters of a subdivision, is a small town 34 miles due east of Gōrakhpur. Beal gives the following variants for the name of the town where Buddha died:—Kuçinagara, Kuçinagari, Kuçanagara, Koçagrāmaka and Kuçinārā (*Buddhist Records of the Western World*, II, 31).

[2] Dr. Waddell's views are expressed in a letter dated 12th March 1893, communicated to me by Dr. Hoey.

1

are nevertheless interesting memorials of the past and well deserving of preservation and thorough exploration[1].

[1] I have thought it advisable to use the system of transliteration recently adopted by the Asiatic Society of Bengal, although I do not approve of some of its details.

For the Dévanâgari alphabet and for all alphabets related to it—

व *a,* वा *â,* इ *i,* ई *î,* उ *u* ऊ *û,* ऋ *r,* ॠ *r* ऌ *l,* ए *e,* ऐ *ê,*

ओ *o,* औ *ô,* उ *ai,* ओ *au,* ·*ṁ,* : *ḥ*

क *k,* ख *kh* ङ *g,* घ *gh,* ङ *ṅ,*

च *c,* छ *ch,* ज *j,* झ *jh,* ञ *ñ,*

ट *ṭ,* ठ *ṭh,* ड *ḍ,* ढ *ḍh,* ण *ṇ,*

त *t,* थ *th,* द *d,* ध *dh,* न *n,*

प *p,* फ *ph,* ब *b,* भ *bh,* म *m.*

य *y,* र *r,* ल *l,* व *v,* (ळ *l)*

श *ṡ,* ष *ṣ,* स *s,* ह *h,*

In the above the *virâma* has been omitted for the sake of clearness. I have substituted *ṅ* as the representative of the guttural nasal for the special character used by the Asiatic Society, which is not in the Government Press fount.

In Modern Vernaculars only, ड़ may be represented by *r* and ढ़ by *rh.*

Avagraha is to be represented by an apostrophe, thus, सोऽपि *so'pi. Visarga* is represented by *ḥ, Anusvâra* is represented by *ṁ,* thus, संशय *saṁṡaya,* and *swandsika* by the sign ~ over the letter nasalised ; thus वाँ *â,* वाँ *â,* and so on .

II.—THE REMAINS NEAR KASIĀ.

THE ruins near Kasiā were first noticed by Buchanan-Hamilton, who visited the place in or about 1810 A. D., and recorded a brief description, which was subsequently published by Mr. Montgomery Martin in *Eastern India*[1].

In 1837 they attracted the attention of Mr. D. Liston, who published an independent short description in the *Journal of the Asiatic Society of Bengal*[2].

Sir Alexander Cunningham's visit took place during the cold season of 1861-62, and Mr. Carlleyle's excavations and restorations were carried on during the years 1875-77.

Since the close of Mr. Carlleyle's operations Dr. Hoey has effected some small clearances.

The extant ruins near Kasiā all lie to the south of the Gorakhpur road, and may be arranged in six groups, as follows :—

(1) an isolated massive brick *stūpa*, known as Dēvïsthān, or Rāmabhār Bhawānī, situated on the western edge of the Rāmabhār Tāl, nearly a mile from Kasiā, in an almost exactly south-western direction ;

(2) a very small mound of ruins, a short distance to the north-east of the village Anrudhwā (*alias* Amrudhwā, or Anraudhā), and about half a mile from the Rāmabhār *stūpa*, a little to the west of south-west ;

(3) the great mound, known as *Māthā Kūar kā Koṭ*, or the Fort of Māthā Kūar, including the ruins of a large *stūpa*, the temple with the colossal recumbent image of the Dying Buddha, a monastery, and many subsidiary buildings. This great mound lies about 1,600 yards west-north-west from the Rāmabhār *stūpa* ;

(4) a colossal statue of the seated Buddha situated about 1,100 feet from the great *stūpa* of the Koṭ in a south-westerly direction. The foundations of the small temple which enshrined this statue still exist to the east of the image. This colossal statue is known locally as Māthā Kūar, and gives its name to the adjoining mound of ruins ;[3]

(5) the remains of a brick enclosing wall. This wall has been for the most part dug up by the cultivators, but can be distinctly traced on the west as far north as a point opposite the western end of the Koṭ, and

[1] Montgomery Martin, *History, Antiquities, Topography and Statistics of Eastern India.*—Three volumes, 8vo., London, 1838. This excellent work, which was printed from Buchanan-Hamilton's manuscript collections, was published by Mr. Martin under his own name. The notice of Kasiyā (Kasiya) will be found at page 357 of Vol. II. Plate 2 (A, B, C) gives a rough sketch on a small scale of the Māthā Kūar mound ; and plate 2 (D) gives a good drawing of the colossal seated statue of Māthā Kūar.

[2] *Notice of a colossal Alto-Relievo, known by the name of Mata Koōr, situated near Kasvia Tumsah, in pergunnah Sidowa, Eastern Division of Gorukhpur District.*—By D. Liston, Esq. (*Journal, Asiatic Society, Bengal*, June, 1837, Volume VI, pages 477-479.) James Prinsep at once identified the colossal seated image as one of Buddha.

[3] The word *Māthā* cannot possibly mean "dead," as supposed by Cunningham, who translates the local name of the monument as "The Dead Prince." He certifies that the spelling *Māthā* is correct. (*Reports*, I, 80) Mr. R. Burn, C.S., the Sub-divisional officer, informs me that the ordinary spelling is Māthā Kūar (माथा कूअर), but that the patwāri and Qānūngo prefer the spelling Mahthā (मइथा). The colossal recumbent statue has now received the local name of Bedhā Kūar, a corruption of Buddha. Although the local people write the word Kūar with the *awerdra*, the actual nasalization is the *anundsika*, of which the sign is accordingly used throughout.

on the south to a point distant 380 feet from the colossal seated statue. The western wall is 520 feet west of that statue.

(6) a number of low earthen mounds or barrows, known locally as *Bhimu-wal*, scattered over the plain to the north and east of the Kōṭ.

The last three items in the above list may be disposed of in few words.

The colossal image of the seated Buddha (No. 4) is a well-executed mediæval work, and is described as follows by Cunningham :—

"The statue, which is made of the dark blue stone of Gayā, is split into two pieces from top to bottom, and is otherwise much injured. The short inscription on its pedestal has been almost worn out by the villagers in sharpening their tools, but the few letters which remain are sufficient to show that the statue is not of older date than the 11th or 12th century. The figure itself is colossal, and represents Buddha, the ascetic, seated under the Bodhi tree at Buddha Gayā. The whole sculpture is 10½ feet in height by 4½ feet in breadth. The height of the figure alone is 5 feet 4½ inches, the breadth across the shoulders being 3 feet 8¾ inches, and across the knees 4 feet 5 inches." [1]

It would be more correct to say that the statue represents Buddha seated under the Bodhi tree after he had attained the rank of Buddha, and had done with austerities. The work shows him attended by Padmapāṇi and other celestial beings, and is a good example of mediæval art.

Mr. Carlleyle, in 1875-76, excavated the mound east of the image, and laid bare the foundations of a small brick temple, containing the remains of a brick pedestal against the western wall on which the statue had apparently once rested. Outside the walls of the temple Mr. Carlleyle found a large slab of black stone with an inscription in characters supposed to date from the eleventh century A.D.

The inscription, which was imperfect, is said to have begun with the words—

Ōm. Namō Buddhāya, namō Buddhāya bhikṣuṇē.

Mr. Carlleyle, as usual, does not inform his readers what was done with this inscription. His reports note a considerable number of interesting objects as found at Kasiā, but rarely indicate how they were disposed of. They are not in the Indian Museum, Calcutta. (See *post*, p. 25.)

Buddhism, long after it was extinct in most parts of India, continued to flourish in the dominions of the Pāla kings of Magadha, which extended from Benares to the mouths of the Ganges. It is impossible to say at exactly what date Buddhism finally disappeared from Eastern India, but it probably had some votaries as late as A.D. 1300 or even 1400[2] ; and certainly had a large number of adherents during the eleventh and twelfth centuries.

Dr. Hoey found a Buddhist inscription, dated (Vikrama) Saṁvat 1176 (=A.D. 1119-20) at Sēt, the reputed site of Çrāvastī. [3]

Other indications of a late survival of Buddhism near Kasiā will be noticed subsequently.

[1] *Archæological Survey Report*, Volume I, page 79.

[2] *Reports*, Vol. XVIII, p. 56.

[3] For accounts of the Pāla kings and their successors, see Cunningham in *Reports*, s. v. " Pāla dynasty of Magadha and Bengal" in *Indra*, especially Volume XI, page 181 ; and Umes Chandar Battacyal in *Journal, Asiatic Society, Bengal*, for 1604, page 99. I greatly doubt the correctness of the accepted identification of the site of Çrāvastī. I have a strong suspicion that Çrāvastī should be identified with Chārdā, or Chahārdah, in the Bahraich district, about forty miles north-west of Sēt-mahēt (Sāhet mahēt). The latter place, which is commonly reputed to be the site of Çrāvastī, will probably prove to be Sāvatya, which was situated eastward from Çrāvastī. (Hardy, *Manual of Buddhism*, 2nd edn., p. 347.) Chārdā is briefly described in *Monumental Antiquities and Inscriptions of the North-Western Provinces and Oudh*, page 203. For the correct name Sēt, see Hoey in *J. As. Soc. Ben.* for 1892, extra number, pp. 2 and 4.

[4] *Journal, Asiatic Society, Bengal*, for 1892, Part I, Extra No., page 57.

The brick wall enclosing on the west and south the grounds in which the *Kōṭ* and the image of the seated Buddha are situated has been mentioned by Carlleyle (*Reports*, XVIII, 96).

The *Bhimuwat* barrows (not *Bhimáwat*, as in *Reports*, I, 79) are certainly very ancient sepulchres. Cunningham counted twenty-one of them, and opened three without result. Carlleyle counted nearly fifty, and found traces of sepulture in two.[1] It is impossible to fix their date, but they probably are to be referred to very remote times, and may be the reason for the sanctity of the locality, and its selection as the site of the Buddhist monuments. These barrows are very inconspicuous, being small mounds varying from three to six feet in height, and from twelve to twenty-five feet in diameter.

At Lauriyā-Navandgaṛh, about fifteen miles north-north-west of Bettiah (which Dr. Waddell supposed to be the site of Kuçanagara), similar, though much larger, barrows exist. A skeleton enclosed in a metal coffin was found on opening one of these barrows. (Cunningham, *Reports*, I, page 70, plate XXIV.)

The Rāmabhār *stūpa* when examined by Cunningham in 1861-62 stood 49 feet above the level of the fields. Cunningham attempted to excavate the *stūpa*, but was stopped by the roots of a large banyan tree. Some years later a district officer (Mr. Lumsden, I believe) made a huge excavation, splitting the building from top to bottom. Nothing was found except a "number of so-called seals" of burnt clay or terra-cotta."[2]

This *stūpa* is undoubtedly an ancient one. Cunningham found at its foot the remains of a miniature *stūpa*, about 16½ feet in diameter, the bricks of which were 17½ inches in length. Bricks of such dimensions are a certain indication of high antiquity. I did not notice the remains of the miniature *stūpa*, and they probably disappeared long ago. The Rāmabhār *stūpa* is quite isolated, and I ascertained that there are no traces of buildings having ever existed near it. The building appears to have been one of the numerous memorial towers erected to commemorate some incident in the sacred history, and not a relic tower.

The little mound of ruins to the north-east of the village of Anrudhwā has been sadly misdescribed by both Cunningham and Carlleyle. Cunningham writes :—

"Between the Fort of Māthā Kūar and the great *stūpa* on the Rāmabhār Jhil, there is a low mound of brick ruins about 500 feet square, which is said to have been a *kōṭ* or fort, and to which no name is given ; but, as it lies close to the village of Anrudhwā on the north-east [misprinted 'north-west'], it may be called the Anrudhwā mound. There is nothing now left to show the nature of the buildings which ever stood on this site; but from the square shape of the ruins, it may be conjectured with some probability that they must be the remains of a monastery. There are three fine *pīpal* trees now standing on the mound." (*Reports*, I, page 79.)

Three pages later Cunningham repeats the erroneous assertion that the ruined mound "is about 500 feet square," and, silently abandoning the monastery theory, decides that the mound must be "the site of the palace of the Mallian kings." His plate XXVI shows the mound as a square "fort" with well-marked elevated sides, each side according to the scale being about 700 to 800 feet.

Carlleyle (*Reports*, XVIII, 92) points out that this mound is more than 800 feet distant from the village, and not only 500 as shown in Cunningham's map, and that the dimensions are "much less than General Cunningham's estimate." Actual measurement gave the length of the eastern and western sides as 170 feet, and that of the northern and southern sides as about 115 feet each. These figures would give an area of 2,166 square yards, but even this calculation is excessive. The mound is in reality an utterly insignificant little heap of ruins composed of small bricks of no great age, situated in No. 231 of the Cadastral Survey map, of which the area is 4 *biswas* 16 *biswānsis*, that is to say, less than quarter of an acre.

It is absolutely impossible that this trivial little mound, which most people would pass without seeing it, could have been either a monastery or a palace.

The villagers say that it was occupied by Bañjāras, an explanation of old ruins often given in this part of the country, and probably correct in this instance.

Cunningham makes another blunder in saying that this mound lies between the Rāmabhār *stūpa* and Māthā Kūar's Kōṭ. It really lies about 500 feet south of the line connecting those buildings. I cannot believe that Sir Alexander Cunningham personally visited this little mound. If he had, it would not have been possible for him to misrepresent the facts so completely. This unfortunate accumulation of misstatements about the Anrudhwā mound has played a large part in the identification of Kasiā with Kuçanagara.

I now come to the description of the principal and most interesting mass of ruins, the so-called fort, or *kōṭ*, of Māthā Kūar.

This mound, which is situated in *mauza* Bishanpura, measured, when examined by Cunningham in 1861-62, in length about 600 feet from north-west to south-east, and in breadth from 200 to 300 feet. (*Reports*, I, 77). Carlleyle, fourteen or fifteen years later, found that the great mound had been considerably encroached upon and diminished (*ibid*, XVIII, 86). The total length now is about 500 feet, more or less.

The large scale plan drawn by Mr. Abdul Ghanī, tahsildār of Deoria, shows the relative position of the various buildings traceable in the mound[1]. Mr. Carlleyle's plates V and VI in Volume XVIII and III in Volume XXII of the *Reports*, may also be consulted. Cunningham's rough sketch in plate XXVII of Volume I is useless. A similar rough sketch is given in plate II of *Eastern India*.

The eastern end of the kōṭ consists of an almost detached mound (*C*), which seems to me to have probably been the site of a brick temple. A flight of stairs near the north-western corner is still distinctly traceable.[2]

Immediately west of this mound is the great *stūpa*, resting on a double plinth. The east side of the lower plinth, according to Carlleyle (*Reports*, XVIII, 65) measured 92 feet in length, and the height of the plinth from the original level of the ground varied from four to four and a-half feet.

This lower plinth projects three feet eight inches beyond the upper plinth, the height of which, according to Mr. Carlleyle, varies from four feet two inches to five feet six inches.

---

[1] Plate. The map was drawn to the scale of 8 feet to the inch, and has been reduced to the scale of 32 feet.

[2] This mound is very incorrectly delineated in Carlleyle's plate III of Volume XXII of the *Reports*.

The double plinth was constructed to carry two buildings, namely, the great *stûpa* to the east, and the temple enshrining the colossal statue of the Dying Buddha to the west.

The buildings were approached on the western side by an upper and a lower flight of stairs.

The north-western portion of the mound was occupied by extensive quadrangular buildings, almost certainly a monastery.

The foundations of several other minor buildings are also traceable, but considerable excavation would be required to render a detailed description or delineation of them possible.

The incomplete excavations carried out by different people during the last thirty-five years have reached the original level in only a few places. Enough has been exposed to show that the plinth of the great *stûpa* and temple was erected in a court crowded with small votive brick *stûpas* of various dimensions. This court was in part certainly, if not throughout, paved with brick and concrete.

The five small *stûpas* (Nos. 1 to 5) were exhumed by Mr. Carlleyle, and are shown in his plan (plate V of *Reports*, Volume XVIII). The group of seventeen little *stûpas* (*E*) at the north-east corner was excavated by Dr. Hoey. Only one of these is shown in Carlleyle's plan. Several *stûpas* flanked the stairs to the west. One of these (No. 7) is nearly 13 feet in diameter.

The great *stûpa* itself has been pretty well extricated from the rubbish which long concealed the greater part of the building, and the circular neck is now fully exposed and easily accessible by a little clambering. No trace of the pilasters noticed by Mr. Carlleyle (*Reports*, XVIII, 79) now remains.

The diameter of the base of the *stûpa* is about 58 feet (58¼ according to Carlleyle) and the height of the topmost point of the ruined core of the dome was about 58 feet above the original ground level in 1875. It is now somewhat less, because Mr. Carlleyle removed some bricks at the top to prevent risk of damage to the temple, which he calls the temple of the Nirvâna. He estimates that the total height of the building when complete "did not exceed 150 feet" (*ibid*, page 80). Cunningham (*Reports*, I, 77) thought that the total height of the *stûpa* above the plain had not exceeded 85 feet. Mr. Abdul Ghani guesses the original elevation to have been about 100 feet. The estimate of 150 feet is certainly a great exaggeration.

There is no doubt that the *stûpa*, the ruins of which are now standing, is a reconstruction of a much older building. This fact was perceived by Cunningham (I, 77), and is fully demonstrated by Carlleyle (XVIII, 74), who found "huge bricks, ornamentally carved with beautiful devices completely hidden in the very centre of the mass of masonry." I also saw some of these bricks embedded in the existing tower. Carlleyle argues with probability from differences in the sizes of the bricks used that the *stûpa* has been twice reconstructed, and that the building which we now see is the third one erected on the site. He assumes that the earliest structure dated from the age of Açôka in the third century B. C. The large size of the oldest bricks (about 14 inches in length) indicates that the original structure was of early date, though not necessarily as early as Açôka. That emperor has obtained credit for more buildings than any sovereign could possibly have erected.

The temple (called by Carlleyle the temple of the Nirvâna) in which the colossal statue of the Dying Buddha is enshrined, stands on the same plinth as the *stûpa*, and at a distance of about 13 feet to the west of it. The story of the discovery of the colossus buried under a mass of rubbish fallen from the ruined *stûpa* is told by Carlleyle (XVIII, 57). That gentleman rebuilt the temple and restored the statue at an expense to himself of about Rs. 1,200 (XXII, 24).

The temple consists of an oblong chamber, just large enough to contain the statue and its pedestal, with enormously thick walls. The entrance faces west, and is approached through an antechamber. When the temple was excavated the walls, though much damaged, were found standing. The roof had been crushed in, but sufficient traces of it remained to show that it was a pointed arch constructed in the Hindu manner with bricks set on edge. Carlleyle, following these indications, reconstructed the roof, and inserted windows in the north and south ends. He also erected a tiled roof over the antechamber, which has disappeared. The roof of the temple is still in tolerably good repair.

The statue when discovered was broken into many fragments. The material is said to be sandstone. Carlleyle recovered as many fragments as possible, and when fragments were not available, he did not hesitate to make up the deficiencies with stones and Portland cement. He also painted and coloured the statue, and ultimately left it in his opinion, "perhaps even better than ever it was" (XVIII, 58, XXII, 18). Within the last two or three years Burmese pilgrims have covered the whole image from head to foot with gold leaf.

The *singhâsan*, or pedestal, on which the image lies, was repaired with equal liberality. Three small human figures are carved on the east side of the pedestal facing the entrance, and below them is an inscription in two lines, about which Carlleyle printed much nonsense (XVIII, 59). An ink impression was submitted to Dr. Fleet, who has published the following correct account of the record:—

" The inscription is below the figure of a man, sitting in a squatting position, on the lower part of the western side of the pedestal of a colossal stone statue of Buddha, recumbent, in the act of attaining *nirvâṇa*, which was found by Mr. Carlleyle in the course of excavations in a large mound of ruins at this village [Kasiâ].

The writing, which covers a space of about 1′ 3¾″ broad by 2¾″ high, is in a state of very good preservation, except that the name of the sculptor is partly illegible in line 2. The average size of the letters is about ₁⁶″. The characters belong to the northern class of alphabets. The language is Sanskrit; and the whole inscription is in prose. The orthography presents nothing calling for remark.

The inscription does not refer itself to the reign of any king, and is not dated; on palaeographical grounds, however, it may be allotted to about the end of the fifth century A.D. It is a Buddhist inscription; and the object of it is to record the gift, by a *mahâvihârasvâmin* named Haribala, of the figure below which it is engraved.

TEXT.

1. *Dêya-dharmô-yam mahâvihârasvâminô Haribalasya.*
2. *Pratimâc-êyam ghatitâ Dinê ... mâ (?) çvarêṣa*

TRANSLATION.

' This (is) the appropriate religious gift of the *mahâvihârasvâmin* Haribala. And this image has been fashioned by Dinê -- mâçvara (?) ' " [1]

[1] *Gupta Inscriptions (Corpus Inscr. Ind.,* Vol. III, p. 272; No. 60; Plate XL, C). Carlleyle professes to print Fleet's version (*Reports,* XVIII, 60), but, as usual, incorrectly.

It is quite possible that this inscription may be as early as A. D. 400. The technical term *mahdvihárasvámin* may be translated Abbot or Superior.

Carlleyle has given a number of minute measurements (*Reports*, XVIII, 99—101). I quote the principal measurements of the temple and recumbent colossus.

Temple.

					Ft.	In.
1.	Outer length at base, north and south				47	8
2.	„ breadth „ north end		...		32	0
3.	„ „ „ south „		...		31	6
4.	Thickness of wall	...	...		9	9
5.	Inner length of chamber		...		30	8
6.	„ breadth „ ...		...		11	9

Antechamber or Vestibule.

					Ft.	In.
1.	Outer length	...	...	...	35	11
2.	„ width	...	...	...	14	7
3.	Thickness of wall	...	...	about	5	0
4.	Inner length	...	...	...	26	2
5.	„ width	...	...	...	10	7

Recumbent Colossus.

					Ft.	In.
1.	Length of pedestal	...	...	...	23	9
2.	Width „	...	...	...	5	6
3.	Length of statue	...	...	...	20	0

A brick bench, fourteen inches in height, said to be part of the original structure, runs along the inside of the front and end walls of the antechamber.

The temple is adorned on the outside with a terra-cotta cornice, or moulding, which is in its original position, about 4½ feet from the floor.

Some sculptures (including a Buddha from Rudrapur, with an imperfect mediæval inscription ; see *Reports*, XVIII, 49) are collected at the entrance. A slab, measuring about 2½ × 1¼", covered with very peculiar symbols, is let into the antechamber wall at the left side of the temple entrance. It is said to be in its original position.

III.—KUÇANAGARA.

I SHALL not attempt in this paper to settle affirmatively the question as to the site of Kuçanagara. I believe that the question is ripe, or very nearly ripe, for settlement, and hope that a final and satisfactory decision will soon be attained.

At present I propose to go into the question only so far as is necessary for the criticism of the generally accepted theory that Kasiá represents Kuçanagara.

I have described the remains which now exist near Kasiá, and now proceed to state the known facts concerning the topography of the ancient town of Kuçanagara.

Our principal authority is the celebrated, learned, and accurate Chinese traveller Hiuen Tsiang, who visited the spot between A. D. 630 and 640.

He describes the *stûpa* built over the cinders from the funeral pyre of the Buddha, and proceeds to say :—

" From this, going north-east through a great forest, along a dangerous and difficult road where wild oxen and herds of elephants and robbers and hunters cause incessant trouble to travellers, after leaving the forest we come to the kingdom of Kiu-shi-naki'o-lo (Kuçinagara). [1]

The capital of this country is in ruins, and its towns and villages waste and desolate. The brick foundation walls of the old capital are about 10 *li* in circuit [*i.e.*, 1⅔ mile]. There are few inhabitants, and the avenues of the town are deserted and waste. At the north-east angle of the city gate is a *stûpa* which was built by Açôka Râja. [2] This is the old home of Canda (Chun-t'o) ; in the middle of it is a well which was dug at the time when he was about to make his offering (*to Buddha*). Although it has overflown for years and months, the water is still pure and sweet.

To north-west of the city 3 or 4 *li* [*i.e.*, ½ to ¾ mile], crossing the Ajitavatî (' O-shi-to-fa-tî) river, on the western bank, not far. we come to a grove of *çâla* trees. The *çûla* tree is like the *hub* tree, with a greenish white bark, and leaves very glistening and smooth. [3]

In this wood are four trees of an unusual height, which indicate the place where Tathâgata died.

There is here a great brick *vihâra* in which is a figure of the *Nirvâṇa* of Tathâgata. He is lying with his head to the north as if asleep. By the side of this *vihâra* is a *stûpa* built by Açôka Râja ; although in a ruinous state, yet it is some 200 feet in height. Before it is a stone pillar to record the *Nirvâṇa* of Tathâgata ; although there is an inscription on it, yet there is no date as to year or month. . . .

By the side of the *vihâra*, and not far from it is a *stûpa*. This denotes the place where Bodhisattva, when practising a religious life, was born as the king of a flock of pheasants. . . . This *stûpa* is still called " the extinguishing fire *stûpa*." . . .

By the side of this, not far off, is a *stûpa*. On the spot Bodhisattva, when practising a religious life, being at that time a deer, saved (*or rescued*) living creatures . . .

To the west of this place, not far off, is a *stûpa*. This is where Subhadra (Shen-hien) died (*entered Nirvâṇa*) . . . . Beside the (*stûpa* of) Subhadra's *Nirvâṇa* is a *stûpa* ; this is the place where the Vajrapâṇi fell fainting on the earth . . The Mallas, with their diamond maces [*vajra*] . . . fell prostrate on the earth . . . By the side where the diamond (*mace-holders*) fell to the earth is a *stûpa*. This is the place where for seven days after Buddha had died they offered religious

[1] The distance, it will be observed, is calculated to the kingdom, not to the capital.

[2] The *Life* has :—" Within the city at north-east angle is a *stûpa* built by Açôka-râja on the site of the old house of Canda."

[3] The *çûla* or *sûla* tree (शाल, साल) is the well-known timber tree, the *sâl* or *sâkhu* (*Shorea robusta*), still abundant in the Gôrakhpur forests. In the *Life* the distance is expressed in slightly different terms :—" Three or four *li* to the north-west of the town we cross the 'O-shi-to-fa-ti (Ajitavatî) river. Not far from the bank of the river we come to a çâla grove." (*Beal, Life of Hiuen Tsiang, p. 97*).

offerings . . . . . To the north of the city, after crossing the river, and going 300 paces or so, there is a *stûpa*. This is the place where they burnt the body of Tathâgata . . . . . Passing the golden river (Kin-ho) to the north, they filled the coffin up with scented oil, &c." . . . By the side of the place of cremation is a *stûpa* ; here Tathâgata, for Kâçyapa's sake, revealed his feet . . .

By the side of the place where he showed his feet is a *stûpa* built by Açoka Râja. This is the place where the eight kings shared the relics. In front is a stone pillar on which is written an account of this event . . . . .

To the south-west of the relic-dividing *stûpa*, going 200 *li* or so [*i. e.*, about 34 miles], we come to a great village ; here lived a Brahman of eminent wealth and celebrity . . . .

Going 500 *li* [*i. e.*, about 84 miles] through the great forest, we come to the kingdom of P'o-lo-ni-sse (Banâras).[1]'

The annexed sketch map shows in a convenient form the relative position of the notable objects described by the traveller.

The town was a small one, only 10 *li*, or about 1¾ mile in circuit, and consequently little more than half a mile across. This statement of Hiuen Tsiang is confirmed by the tradition of the protests made by the faithful attendant of Buddha to his selection of so obscure a place as Kuçanagara for his departure from the world. Why, he asked, die in a "poor village, this sandhole, this straggling village, this suburb, this semblance of a town," when the six great cities of Çrâvastî, Sakêta, Campa, Varânasi, Vaisâlî, and Râjagriha were all longing for the honour of witnessing the departure of the Master ? (Rookhill, *Life of the Buddha*, page 136.)

The town, though small and of no account when compared with the magnificent royal cities enumerated by Ânanda, the ruins of each of which to this day cover many miles, was yet encircled with brick walls, and the foundations of these walls and the ruined streets could still be traced in the seventh century of our era.

The river Ajitavatî (called Hiranyavatî in other books), flowed to the north and west of the town. A tope, or *stûpa* (No. 1), built by Açoka, stood "at the north-east angle of the city gate." The grove of *sâl* trees in which the Master passed away stood to the north-west of the town, at a distance of from half to three-quarters of a mile from it, across the river. At, or close to, this grove was the temple of the Nirvâṇa containing a statue of Buddha, "lying with his face to the north, as if asleep." (No. 2) Close to this temple was a great *stûpa* of Açoka (No. 3), which, though ruinous in the pilgrim's time, was still about 200 feet high. An inscribed stone pillar (No. 4) was beside this great monument, and not far off were two more *stûpas* (Nos. 5 and 6). The *stûpa* of Subhadra (No. 7) was to the west, not far off. Two more *stûpas* (Nos. 8 and 9) were in the same locality.

To the north of the city, 300 paces or so beyond the river, a *stûpa* (No. 10) marked the place of the Master's cremation, and in the same direction were two more *stûpas* (Nos. 11 and 12), and a second inscribed stone pillar (No. 13).

The sacred buildings, therefore, fall into three distinct blocks. The first consisted of a single edifice, the ancient *stûpa* of Açoka to the north-east of the city gate, on the southern side of the river. The second group consisting of eight monuments was on the other side of the river, to the north-west of the town, and consisted of a great

---

[1] *Records of Western Countries*, Volume II, pages 31—43. The reader should observe that the distance given is again to the kingdom, not to the city. Much of the difficulty in interpreting the Chinese pilgrims' itineraries is due to their habit of frequently reckoning distances to kingdoms or countries, and not to cities. Unfortunately we do not know where the frontiers of any kingdom should be placed in the fifth and seventh centuries A. D.

NORTH.

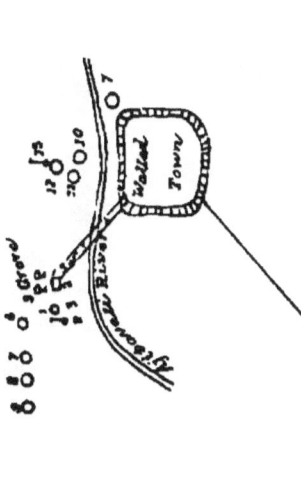

KEY.

No. 1. Aśoka's stúpa at north-east angle of city gate.*
„ 2. Vihára of Nirvána.
„ 3. Stúpa of Aśóka.
„ 4. Stone pillar recording Nirvána.
„ 5. Fire-extinguishing stúpa.
„ 6. Life-rescuing stúpa.
„ 7 Stúpa of Subhadra.
„ 8. Vajrapáni stúpa.
„ 9. Stúpa of religious offerings.
„ 10. Cremation stúpa.
„ 11. Revolution of foot stúpa.
„ 12. Relic-dividing stúpa.
„ 13. Relic-dividing pillar.

* According to the Life, No. 1 was inside the walls.

Scale—1 inch to mile : 8 li to mile.

temple or monastery containing a recumbent image,[1] six *stúpas*, including one of vast dimensions, and an inscribed stone pillar. All these structures were near the grove in which Buddha died. The third group of buildings stood to the north of the town, less than a quarter of a mile across the river, and consisted of three *stúpas* and an inscribed pillar marking the scene of the cremation.

The account given by the earlier Chinese pilgrim, Fa-hian, who visited the place about A.D. 405, is not nearly so full as that of Hiuen Tsiang, and differs from it in some details. An examination of the points of agreement and difference is instructive, and will help the student of the pilgrims' works to appreciate the value of their topographical information.

Fa-hian places Kuçanagara twelve *yójanas* to the east of the Charcoal tope, where the cinders from the pyre were enshrined. Hiuen Tsiang gives the bearing as north-east, not east, but does not specify the distance along the "dangerous and difficult road." I have no doubt that the bearing given by the later and more observant traveller is the more correct, and that Fa-hian used the words "still to the east" very loosely, being indifferent whether the bearing was due east, south-east, or north-east. It is easy to prove that this degree of laxity of expression is habitual to Fa-hian.

The omission of Hiuen Tsiang to specify the distance is probably due to the dangers and difficulties of the road in his time, which rendered exact calculation of distances troublesome. In Fa-hian's time the road was probably more open.

Fa-hian, with his usual indifference to accurate expression of direction, places the grove of *sál* trees where Buddha died on the north of the town. Hiuen Tsiang places the grove to the north-west.

The town, which was almost quite deserted in the seventh century, had still a small monastic population in the fifth.

"In the city," says Fa-hian, "the inhabitants are few and far between, comprising only the families belonging to the different societies of monks."

The earlier traveller mentions specifically only five of the notable spots included in his successor's list. The five are :—

    (1) the scene of Buddha's death;

    (2) the spot where Subhadra attained to wisdom;

    (3) the spot where offerings were made to Buddha in his coffin for seven days;

    (4) the spot where the Vajrapáni laid aside his golden club; and

    (5) the spot where the relics were divided.

These correspond to the grove and the monuments Nos. 2, 7, 8 and 9 in Hiuen Tsiang's list, and all belong to the north-western group. Fa-hian makes no mention of the northern group of buildings, or of the *stúpa* of Açóka north-east of the city gate.[2]

There is no real discrepancy between the accounts of the two pilgrims.

---

[1] The term *vihára* (विहार, or बीहार) may mean either a temple or a monastery. Hiuen Tsiang's phrase "a great brick *vihára*, in which is a figure of the Nirvána of Tathágata" appears to refer to a temple rather than to a monastery. No monastery at Kuçanagara is distinctly mentioned by Hiuen Tsiang, though the earlier traveller Fa-hian in the fifth century found *sanghárámas*, or monasteries, still existing, and occupied by a few monks.

[2] My quotations are from the latest version of Fa-hian's *Travels*, that of Professor Legge (Oxford, 1886), page 70. This translation, although it corrects its predecessors in several particulars, seems to be little known, and is rarely quoted. References is usually made to Mr. Beal's revised version in Volume I of *Buddhist Records of the Western World* (Boston, 1885; in Trübner's Oriental Series). In the passage discussed in the text the versions of both scholars substantially agree. The only difference of any moment is that Mr. Beal transliterates the name of the river as Hiranyavatí, whereas Professor Legge transliterates the name as Nairañjaná, and remarks in a note "confounded, according to Eitel, even by Hiuen Chwang [Hiuen Tsiang], with the Hiranyavatí, which flows past the city on the south." According to Klaproth the Chinese word in Fa-hian's text is *Hi-lian*, and in other Chinese works it is called *Shi-lai-na-fa-ti*, or *Savarnavatí*, which is synonymous with *Hiranyavatí*.

IV.—THE SUPPOSED IDENTITY OF KASIÅ AND KUÇANAGARA.

I am now in a position to examine the arguments which convinced Sir Alexander Cunningham, and his Assistant Mr. Carlleyle, that the ruins near Kasiå are those of the ancient Kuçanagara. The identification was made so positively by these authorities, and with such an apparent show of reason, that it has been usually accepted without demur, and until my visit to Kasiå I entertained no doubt on the subject. No one could be more surprised than I was to find that unprejudiced local investigation proved the identification to be impossible.

In 1883 Sir A. Cunningham wrote :—

" Mr. Carlleyle's great work of the season was the complete exploration of the ruins at Kasiå, which I had already identified with the ancient city of Kuçinagara, where Buddha died......By his patient and methodical explorations at Kasiå Mr. Carlleyle has fixed its identification beyond all doubt. On the west side of the great stúpa be discovered the famous Nirvána statue of Buddha, just as it was described by the Chinese pilgrim, Hiuen Tsiang. It is quite certain that this statue is the same that was seen by the pilgrims, as there is an inscription on the pedestal of the mourning figure, beside the couch, of two lines in characters of the Gupta period. The figure is colossal, 20 feet in length, and is represented lying on the right side with the right hand under the head, and facing to the west precisely as described by Hiuen Tsiang. The statue was enshrined in a vaulted temple, the vault being constructed in the old Hindu fashion, such as is found in the great temple of Mahábódhi at Buddha Gayá. In this construction the radiating voussoirs are placed edge to edge, instead of face to face.

Altogether the identifications in this report mutually support each other, and their positions are well sustained by the two fixed points of Kapilavastu on the west and Kuçinagara on the east."[1]

This extremely positive and confident language used by the official head of the Archæological Survey naturally carried conviction with it, and I am not aware that any doubts as to the identification of Kasiå with Kuçanagara have yet found their way into print.

The argument employed by Cunningham, in the last sentence of the passage above quoted, was demolished some years ago. His equally confident identification of Kapila-vastu with the remains at Bhuilá in the Basti district is now universally rejected, and was certainly erroneous.[2] The supposed " fixed point " of Kapilavastu therefore disappears, and with it goes the whole series of identifications of places between Bhuilá and Kasiå made by Mr. Carlleyle, which are certainly all wrong. The identification of Kasiå with Kuçanagara must consequently be proved, if at all, by arguments altogether inde-pendent of the supposed site of Kapilavastu.

I cannot now attempt to discuss the geographical position of Kapilavastu and Kuçanagara with reference to the fixed points of Çrávastí, Vaisáli, Rájagriha, and Benares. That discussion would be of a rather complicated character, and would

---

[1] Cunningham's preface to Volume XVIII of the *Archæological Survey Reports*, being Carlleyle's *Report of a Tour in the Gorakhpur district* in 1875-76 and 1876-77.

[2] In 1879 Cunningham wrote in the preface to Volume XII of the *Reports* th t "the result of my examination was the most perfect conviction of the accuracy of Mr. Carlleyle's identification of Bhuilá Tál with the site of Kapilavastu, the famous birthplace of Sákyi Muni." Nevertheless, that identification rested on no substantial grounds. Some of the reasons which prove it to be erroneous have been twice printed by Dr. Führer, *viz.*, in the *Sharqi Architecture of Jaunpur*, Calcutta, 1889, page 69 being Volume I of the *Archæological Reports, new series*, and Volume XI of the *New Imperial Series*; and again in *Monumental Antiquities and Inscriptions in the N.-W. P. and Oudh*, Allahabad, 1891, page 222. This volume is Volume II of the *New Imperial Series*. Many other reasons may be adduced besides those given by Dr. Führer.

require much time and space. I confine myself at present to purely topographical arguments and still undertake to demonstrate that Kasiā cannot possibly represent Kuçanagara.

The identification was originally suggested by Professor H. H. Wilson, and when Cunningham undertook his first tour as Archæological Surveyor in 1861-62, he was willing to believe that Kasiā might prove to be Kuçanagara. After visiting the place in the course of that tour he quickly arrived at the conclusion that the two places must be identical. With his usual disregard of philological principles he had "little doubt that Kasiā should be written Kusiā, with the short u." This conjecture is, of course, of no value as an argument, and it would be difficult to find an example of the change of the labial into the guttural vowel in an accented syllable. The supposed correspondence of Kasiā with Kuçanagara "both in position and name" is therefore reduced to an alleged correspondence in "position" only. The argument as to position (*Reports*, *I*, 80) rests on Cunningham's assumed value for the *yôjana*, and his interpretation of the Chinese pilgrim's observations concerning the relative positions of Kuçanagara, Vaisāli, and Benares. That question, as I have said, I will not now go into, and content myself with remarking that it is not so simple as Cunningham supposed. [1]

At the time of Cunningham's visit in 1861-62, the colossal recumbent statue of Buddha had not been discovered, and the topographical arguments in favour of the identification of Kasiā with Kuçanagara were extremely feeble. Cunningham had to admit that of the various *stûpas* mentioned by Hiuen Tsiang "most have now disappeared." He attempted to explain (*I*, 76) this awkward fact by suggesting that bricks had been removed by the people, and that changes had been caused by "inundations of the Little Gandak river, which at some former period must have flowed close by the sacred buildings of Kuçanagara, as there are several old channels between the two principal masses of ruins, which are still occasionally filled during the rainy season." [2]

Cunningham evidently appreciated the obstacles in the way of the desired identifications caused by the troublesome facts. He again remarks (p. 81) that "owing to the wanderings of the Little Gandak river, it is somewhat difficult to follow Hiuen Tsiang's account of the sacred edifices at Kuçinagara." It is indeed difficult, because the pilgrim's account, though it agrees with the facts of Kasiā in some particulars, is absolutely irreconcilable with them in others. There is no reason whatever to doubt the accuracy of Hiuen Tsiang's account of places which he personally visited, and when his account is inconsistent with local facts, an identification based on an attempt to force the facts into agreement with the account must be rejected. Sir Alexander Cunningham's strong prepossession in favour of the identification of Kasiā with Kuçanagara unfortunately led him, as in the case of Bhuili and Kapilavastu, into an unconscious twisting of the facts. He was naturally much struck by the curious coincidence between the name of the village adjoining the Buddhist ruins near Kasiā and the name of the Buddhist saint Aniruddha, who took a prominent part in the obsequies of the Master. One form of the name of the village is Anrudhwā (अनरुधवा) and the coincidence between that

[1] I hope on another occasion to examine the problem of geographical position. To do so now is unnecessary, and would extend this paper to an unwieldy bulk. The exact site of Crâvasti is not certain (*ante*, p. 8).

[2] By "the two principal masses of ruins" Cunningham means the Kâmabhâr *Stûpa* and the Mâthâ Kûar *Kôṭ*. Channels between these really exist, but there is no channel where Cunningham's theory requires one, namely, between the village of Anrudhwā and the *kôṭ*.

form and Aniruddha (अनिरुद्ध) is indisputable. I also heard the name pronounced as Anraudhā (अनरौधा). On the new Cadastral Survey maps the name is written Amraudhā, with m not n; (अमरौधा), and some people declare that this form is correct. If it is, then the name has nothing to do with Aniruddha. Cunningham did not learn the m form of the name, and considered it:—

"More than probable that the village of Anrudhwa must have received its name from some former memorial of the far-sighted Aniruddha, the cousin of Buddha. In Sheet 102 of the Indian Atlas the name of this village is spelt Aniroodwa, which is more correct than the name written down for me by a Brahman of the place. The existence of this name in the immediate vicinity of the ancient monuments of Kusiá [sic] must I think, add considerable weight to all the other evidence in favour of the identification of Kusiá with the ancient Kusinagara" (I, 84).

The repeated use in this passage of the fictitious name Kusiá is a good illustration of the necessity for caution in reading Cunningham's works.

The ruins called *Máthá Kúar ká Kót* and the colossal seated image of Buddha, called Máthá Kúar, are situated within the limits of *mauza* (townland) Bisanpura. An old man informed me that long ago the lands now known as Bisanpura were included in Anrudhwá.

Cunningham at first "conjectured with some probability" that the buildings which once stood on the site of the mound near Anrudhwá village must have been a monastery (I, 79). Three pages later he arrived at a totally different opinion.

"After a long and attentive comparison of all our available information,"

He writes :—

"I have come to the conclusion that the famous city of Kuçinagara must have occupied the site of the mound and village of Anrudhwá. The ruined mound, which is about 500 feet square, I would identify as the site of the palace of the Mallian kings, which was in the midst of the city, and to [the city itself I would assign an extent of about 1,000 feet on all sides of the palace. This would give a square area of 25,500 feet, or nearly half a mile on each side, with a circuit of 10,000 feet, or nearly 2 miles, as recorded by Hiuen Tsiang" (I, 82).

The mound which on page 79 was "a monastery," has become "the palace of the Mallian kings" on page 82. The utterly insignificant and scarcely visible mound near Anrudhwá is stated to be 500 feet square. In Plate XXVI a fancy plan of this mound is given showing a square fort-like structure including three separate eminences, and about 800 feet square according to the scale. Carlleyle (XVIII, 92) found the measurements of the mound to be about 170×115 feet, which would give an area of 19,550 square feet. The cadastral survey measurement, as already mentioned, gives a smaller area, namely, 4⅔ *biswas*, equivalent to about 10,530 square feet, or less than a quarter of an acre. Cunningham's "square area of 2,500 feet" is, of course, a blunder (500×500=250,000).

Cunningham also misrepresented in his plate the position of this ill-used mound, which is really about 800 feet north-east of the village (*Reports*, XVIII, 92), and not 500 as shown in the plan.

This series of extraordinary errors plainly indicates that Sir Alexander Cunningham did not personally examine the Anrudhwá mound. Many of the erroneous statements which disfigure his *Reports* are due to his unfortunate practice of trusting to the observations and measurements of his native staff, without checking them

5

himself. If he had himself examined the little mound near Anrudhwâ, he must have perceived that it is probably not very old, and that it certainly could not possibly have been the site either of a monastery or a palace.

Hiuen Tsiang, in or about A.D. 635, found the distinct remains of a walled city existing. " The capital of this country," he observes, "is in ruins. . . . . The brick foundation walls of the old capital are about 10 *li* in circuit. There are few inhabitants, and the avenues of the town are deserted and waste." I examined minutely the site and surroundings of the village of Anrudhwâ, and am able to affirm positively that a walled town never at any time existed at or near the village, which presents no sign of antiquity. It is a mere collection of huts. It does not stand on a mound, and there are no broken bricks or pottery, or in fact any signs of ancient habitation, in the adjoining fields. It is absolutely impossible that a walled town, which still existed in a dilapidated condition in the seventh century, should have disappeared without leaving a mound or a fragment of brick. On every ancient site the fields are full of broken brick, and such a site must necessarily be raised above the surrounding country.

Cunningham's plate gives an outline of the " recorded extent of ancient city," extending about 1,000 feet on each side of his imaginary "palace." There is no indication whatever of the existence of buildings round the little mound which he dubbed " the palace of the Mallian kings." A few broken bricks and potsherds may be found in one direction only as far as about 200 yards from the north-west corner of the little mound up to an old well, and that is the only sign of antiquity about Anrudhwâ. No signs of ancient habitation exist between the mound and the Râmabhâr *stûpa* on the edge of the *tâl.* That monument is absolutely isolated.

The fact that no walled town ever existed at or near Anrudhwâ is fatal to the identification of the *Mâthâ Kuar kâ Kôt* with the scene of Buddha's death.

Hiuen Tsiang places the grove where Buddha died, and the eight monuments (Nos. 2 to 9) commemorating the event, to the north-west of the town of Kuçanagara, on the far bank of the Ajitavatî river. The *kôt* of Mâthâ Kuar is to the north-west of Anrudhwâ, and, if the *kôt* is the scene of Buddha's death, Anrudhwâ must represent the walled town. It is quite certain that no walled town ever existed on the site of Anrudhwâ.

Mr. Carlleyle, while correcting several of the blunders in his chief's description, has allowed his own imagination free play, and has dreamed that he could see the traces of the (I) " city proper or secular city," and (II) " an outer city, which might be called the monastic or religious city" (*Reports,* XVIII, 94-97). All that he really saw was the old boundary wall of the grounds surrounding the *kôt.* His " secular city, inhabited by the nobles, the military class, the traders, the artisans, and the labourers, and containing the palace of the Mallian nobles," which is supposed to have been " situated to the south-east, and to have commenced at a point about 1,500 feet to the east of the village of Anrudhwâ, &c.," has not, and never had, any existence save in Mr. Carlleyle's imaginative pages.

The exposure of the mistakes in the *Reports* is tedious, but I must point out that the descriptions given by both Cunningham and Carlleyle, of the old river channels near Kasiâ are extremely confused and untrustworthy. Certainly there is no channel, nor was there ever a channel, between the *kôṭ* and the village of Anrudhwá. The ground between the village and the *kôṭ* is high. The river Ajitavatí certainly flowed between the town of Kuçanagara and the scene of Buddha's death.

If the other conditions for the identification were fulfilled, it would perhaps be possible, though not altogether easy, to find places in the *Máthá Kúar kâ Kôṭ* for the eight monuments described by Hiuen Tsiang as existing near the grove of death. But both Cunningham and Carlleyle have to admit that they can find no trace whatever of the northern group of four monuments (Nos. 11 to 13), three *stûpas* and a pillar, which according to their theory should be traceable between the village of Anrudhwá and the Gôrakhpur road.

As a matter of fact, the only remains in this position are the prehistoric low tumuli already described. Mr. Carlleyle counted nearly fifty of these barrows (XVIII. 94); and it is absurd to suggest that while these have been spared, every trace of the northern group of monuments described by Hiuen Tsiang has been swept away. Both Cunningham and Carlleyle try to give a northern extension to their imaginary town by dragging into it the *Kusmi Pôkhar*, an ordinary tank situated about midway between Kasiá and the *Kôṭ*. This tank presents no marks of antiquity, and there is no reason to suppose that it has any connection with the Buddhist remains.

The various attempts made by both Cunningham and Carlleyle to identify the isolated Rámabhár *stûpa* with any of the monuments described by Hiuen Tsiang are complete failures.

Cunningham wished to identify the Rámabhár building with the cremation *stûpa*, but also thought that it might possibly correspond to the *stûpa* of Açôka "at the north-east angle of the city gate" (I, 84). Carlleyle (XVIII, 90) thought that the Rámabhár edifice must be the cremation *stûpa* (page 90), but on the next page changed his mind, and decided that it could not be the cremation *stûpa*, and might be the 'relic-dividing' *stûpa*. He then proceeded to identify the cremation *stûpa* with "a small low sloping round-topped mound, about 50 feet in diameter, with a large tree growing on the top of it," which he says he found existing 175 feet north-east of the mound near Anrudhwá. These wild conjectures are not deserving of serious criticism.

I now proceed to briefly sum up my reasons for maintaining that the remains to the south-west of Kasiá are not only not proved to be, but are proved not to be, those of the ancient Kuçanagara.

(1) The existing remains are not at Kasiá, but at a considerable distance from it. There is no reason whatever to suppose that the name Kasiá has any connection with the name Kuçanagara or Kusinârâ, while there are excellent reasons for supposing that there is no such connection; nor have the ruins any necessary connection with the modern town of Kasiá.

(2) The value of the *yôjana* is very uncertain, and the interpretation of the evidence as to the geographical position of Kuçanagara is, both on account of the uncertain value of the *yôjana*, and for many other reasons, a very obscure problem. [1]

---

[1] I am prepared to demonstrate that owing to its geographical position Kasiá cannot possibly be Kuçanagara, but the proof must be reserved for another occasion.

(3)   The identification by Cunningham and Carlleyle of Bhuilä in the
Basti district with Kapilavastu has been proved to be erroneous,
and all the identifications of places between Kapilavastu and Kuçanagara made by the same writers are necessarily erroneous also, and
the proved erroneousness of these identifications renders the identification of Kasiä with Kuçanagara highly improbable.

(4)   The topography of Kuçanagara is minutely described by Hiuen Tsiang,
as it was in or about A.D. 635.   If the remains near Kasiä are those
which adjoined Kuçanagara, then the village of Anrudhwä must
correspond with the fortified town of Kuçanagara ; a river must have
flowed between that village and the *Mäthä Kúar kä Kól* ; traces
should be visible of a group of monuments north of the town, as well
as of another to the north-west ; and there should be a *stúpa* at the
north-east angle of the city gate.   None of these conditions are
satisfied at Kasiä.

(5)   The great *stúpa* at Kuçanagara was, even when ruinous in the time
of Hiuen Tsiang, still about 200 feet high.   The great *stúpa* near
Kasiä was probably never more than 85 feet high, according to
Cunningham's estimate (I, 77).   Carlleyle's estimate of 150 feet as
the maximum possible height is absurd.   Consequently the great *stúpa*
on the *Mäthä Kúar kä Kól* cannot be the great *stúpa* of Kuçanagara.

Mr. Carlleyle, when he went to Kasiä in 1875-76, candidly admitted (XVIII, 55)
that the identification with Kuçanagara " up to that time could not be said to be absolutely certain. "   His real reason for deciding that the identification was absolutely certain is his remarkable discovery of the colossal recumbent statue of the Dying
Buddha.

Mr. Carlleyle had before him the words of Hiuen Tsiang :—" There is here a great
brick *vihära*, in which is a figure of the Nirväna of Tathägata.   He is lying with his
head to the north as if asleep.   By the side of this *vihära* is a *stúpa* built by Açöka
Räja ; although in a ruinous state, yet it is some 200 feet in height. "

Mr. Carlleyle, assuming that the site was that of Kuçanagara, and the *stúpa* on the
kól was that mentioned by Hiuen Tsiang, excavated a protuberance on the mound near
the *stúpa* in the hope that he " might possibly have the good fortune here to hit upon
some remains of the famous statue. "(XVIII, 57).   After digging to the depth of about
ten feet he actually came on the thigh of the recumbent colossus now exhibited, and he
gradually exposed the whole of the enclosing shrine with its antechamber, both of which
he subsequently repaired and restored.

The discovery of this great image, " just as it was described by the Chinese pilgrim, Hiuen Tsiang," seemed to Sir Alexander Cunningham and Mr. Carlleyle conclusive
proof of the desired identification.   The coincidence that, while the explorer was look-
ing for a " Nirväna statue," his pickaxe should actually strike one, is unquestionably
curious and startling.   But it is very far from being the conclusive proof which Cunningham and Carlleyle imagined it to be.

The attitude of an image of the dying Buddha was fixed by rigid convention, and
never varied.   Every such image must correspond to the description given by the

Chinese pilgrim as "lying with his head to the north as if asleep." Consequently, unless such an image existed at Kuçanagara only, the discovery of it could not prove the place where it was found to be Kuçanagara. But it is well known that the image of the dying Buddha was a favourite subject of Buddhist art from Kābul to Burmah. Several examples of it on a small scale are known among the Græco-Roman sculptures from the Yusufzai or Gandhāra country, and I have elsewhere shown that the motive is copied from Græco-Roman sarcophagi. [1] Colossal statues of the Dying Buddha are still numerous in Burmah, where they are known to occur more than 100 feet in length. I am not aware of the discovery of any example, except the Kasiá one, in India Proper, but it is extremely probable that such statues existed and that some of them will be found. Sir Alexander Cunningham has himself suggested that the so-called Nine-yard (naugaza) graves, which exist at Ajōdhya and in many other places, and are variously ascribed to one of the patriarchs, or to some Musalman saint, mark the positions of colossal images of the Dying Buddha. As Dr. Waddell observes, "such images were usual at great relic shrines," and the existence of one at Kasiá no more proves that place to be the scene of Buddha's death, than the existence of one at Rangoon entitles that city to claim the honour. [2]

[1] *Græco-Roman Influence on the Civilisation of Ancient India (Journal, Asiatic Society of Bengal,* Volume LVIII, Part I, 1800, page 196). " Es gehört zu den geistvollsten Vermutungen von Vincent A. Smith, die Vorlage zu dieser soudrock-vollsten Komposition der alten buddhistischen Kunst seien griechische und römische Sarcophagreliefs gewesen." (A. Grünwedel, *Buddhistische Kunst in Indien,* Berlin, 1893, page 100).

[2] The so-called " giant's grave " at Gopālganj, four miles north of Dinājpur in Bengal, is 57 feet long. Another similar tomb exists a mile south of Dinājpur. (*List of Ancient Monuments in Bengal,* Calcutta, 1896, p. 164.) Naugaza tombs are numerous in the Rohtak district of the Panjáb (Cunningham, *Reports,* XVI, 137).

V.—CONSERVATION.

THE question will naturally be asked :—Granting that the site of Kuçanagara has not yet been found, what holy place do the remains near Kasiá correspond to, and are they worth preserving, although they do not mark the scene of Buddha's death?

I am not disposed to add another to the mass of rash and ill-considered identifications which have done so much to obscure the study of early Indian history, but I may venture to say this much that, if the ruins near Kasiá were visited by the Chinese pilgrims, they may mark the spot where a *stúpa* was erected over the charcoal or ashes taken from Buddha's funeral pyre. Fa-hian (*Legge*, page 70) places this spot four *yójanas* east of the place where Buddha sent back his horse. He gives no description, but simply mentions "the charcoal tope, where there is also a monastery."[1] Hiuen Tsiang is, as usual, more communicative, and notes that—

" By the side of the ashes *stúpa* is an old *sanghárama* [monastery], where there are traces of the four former Buddhas, who sat and walked there.

On the right hand and left of this convent there are several hundred *stúpas*, among which is one large one built by Açôka Rája; although it is mostly in ruins, yet its height is still about 100 feet." (*Records*, II, 31.)

The large *stúpa* on the *Máthá Kúar ká Kôț* may well be the Açôka stúpa referred to. Its height was recently 58 feet, and Cunningham himself (I, 77) calculated that its original height was about 85 feet. It cannot possibly have been 150 feet high, as supposed by Carlleyle (XVIII, 80). The great *stúpa* of the Nirvâṇa at Kuçanagara was 200 feet high, even when ruinous in Hiuen Tsiang's time.

My plan actually shows 28 *stúpas*, small and great, now visible at the *Kôț*, and many more would certainly be disclosed by excavation. It is very probable therefore that " several hundreds " once existed in the precincts. Anybody who has visited Buddha Gayá will understand how votive *stúpas* are crowded round holy places.[2] The ruins of a monastery also exist on the Kôț. Though the suggestion that the remains near Kasiá mark the site of the Charcoal Tope seems to me plausible, it requires discussion and verification, and is open to certain objections. I cannot at present insist on it.

If it should prove correct, it will fix the site of Kuçanagara as lying to the northeast of Kasiá across the Gandak either in the Champáran district north or north-northeast of Bettiah, or in Népál. Dr. Waddell has suggested Lauriyá-Navandgaṛh, where there is an Açôka pillar, 15 miles north-north-west of Bettiah, as being the true site of Kuçanagara. But the materials for an exact determination are not at present available. The ancient sites in the northern parts of the Champáran district along the old road

---

[1] Beal calls this monument the "Ashes Tower." Legge points out that the Chinese character is more accurately rendered by the word "charcoal." Remusat has "le tour des charbons," which Laidlay in his version (page 221) translates " The Tower of the Charcoal."

[2] Cunningham (I, 78, observes that the *Kôț* is just such a mass as would have been formed by "the ruin of a considerable number of independent buildings, such as a cluster of *stúpas* of all sizes." Carlleyle says (XVIII, 67) :—" In the course of my general excavations I found a numerous assemblage of very small brick *stúpas* scattered over the eastern half of the great mound." He cleared away several (ib., 70 and XXII, 55).

from Pātaliputra to Nepāl seem to be very numerous,[1] and no one knows what is in Nepāl.

Whatever ancient place the remains near Kasiā may ultimately be identified with, they are of much interest and well worthy of conservation.

I am not aware of any equally well-preserved group of Buddhist remains in these provinces, and am of opinion that the site near Kasiā would repay both excavation and conservation.[2]

The measures required for the conservation of the remains now exposed would be neither difficult nor expensive.

Nothing can be done for the Rāmabhār stūpa. It has been rent from top to bottom by the ill-judged excavations of Mr. Lumsden.

The Māthā Kūar kā Kōt should be declared the property of Government. It has been taken possession of by the Collector (Dr. Hoey) in an informal way, and nobody is allowed to remove bricks from it.

The great stūpa requires some slight repair to make it safe. I would not attempt to restore it, but would simply keep what is left of it standing.

The roof of the temple of the Dying Buddha leaks a little, and should be mended. The door also requires repair.

The tiled roof put by Mr. Carlleyle on the antechamber has fallen in. It is not necessary and need not be replaced.

A Brahman, whom Mr. Carlleyle settled at the place, has erected a small Mahā-dēo at the top of the steps, and derives a trifling income from offerings. He has also been allowed to build himself a good house and make gardens on the mound, as shown in my plan.

He might be kept on as watchman at Rs. 4 a month, and, if necessary, his house and garden could be cleared away, a small sum being paid as compensation. The bungalow and hut built by Mr. Carlleyle should be cleared away, if excavations are undertaken; but the bungalow, with some repair, would be useful during excavation, and need not be cleared away till the last.

A very small sum, say Rs. 100, would suffice for the trifling repairs to the stūpa, etc., which are at present required.

The following inscription on a slab let into the wall behind the Dying Buddha was set up by Mr. Carlleyle:—

"This famous statue and temple of the Nirvāṇa of Buddha were discovered, and along with the adjoining stūpa, excavated and the statue (which was found broken and scattered into numberless fragments) was entirely reconstructed, repaired and restored, and the temple also repaired and roofed in by—

A. C. CARLLEYLE,

Assistant Archæological Surveyor,

Archæological Survey of India."

KUSINAGARA,
March 1877.

---

[1] See the map of the district, and Carlleyle's notes in *Reports*, XXII, pages 47-57. My most recent studies incline me to believe that the site of Kusanagara is to be sought in Nepāl, probably near the upper course of the Rāptī, and about forty miles from Kāthmāndu.

[2] The stūpa at Sarnāth is more perfect, but the group of remains near Kasiā is more interesting, and less damaged.

The word "Kusinagara" should be wholly obliterated. The rest of the inscription may stand, because the temple may be loosely described as one of the Nirvāna, though the strictly correct word to use for the death of Buddha is *parinirvāya*.

No excavations should be allowed except for a definite purpose and under competent direction. If they are undertaken, I should be disposed to begin with the eastern mound (C on my plan), which should be cleared carefully so as to show its nature. I think it is a temple.

I would then clear the base of the plinth of the great *stūpa* on the east and north sides down to the original ground level, carefully preserving any votive *stūpas*, etc., which might come to light.

The excavation should then be continued along the north side of the monastery (D) so as to completely expose its walls, and the internal excavation of the monastery should be carried sufficiently far to disclose its plan. The steps approaching the temple of the Dying Buddha should also be cleared, and, if funds permitted, the space between the temple and the monastery should be opened out. The southern side should be left to the last, and sufficient land outside the mound should be acquired to permit of the deposit of all material excavated. The land is poor and of small value.

Of course, all moveable antiquities found should be carefully preserved with records of their exact find spots, and suitable rewards should be given to the finders.

The antiquities found by Mr. Carlleyle have mostly disappeared. They are not in the Indian Museum, Calcutta. The following is a list of them :—

Number.	Object.	Where found.	Reference.
1	Inscription on large black slab, in characters of 11th century, beginning Ōm. *Namō Buddhāya, namō Buddhāya bhikṣunī.*	In small temple near seated statue called *Māthā Kūar.*	*Reports,* XVIII, 56 }[1] XXII, 18 }
2	Human bones and charred substances ...	Antechamber of temple of Dying Buddha.	Ditto, XVIII, 62
3	Red terracotta figure of Buddha in the attitude of teaching, two feet two inches in height.	At north-east corner of foundation of plinth of great *stūpa.*	Ditto 67
4	Iron bells and rods	East of great *stūpa* ...	Ditto 67
5	Image of Ganēś, in dark greenish-blue stone, 1' 8" high.	Ditto ...	Ditto 67
6	Small sitting figure of woman, called Māyā Dēvī, by Carlleyle, in dark greenish stone.	Embedded in wall inside antechamber of temple.	Ditto 67
7	Small broken figure of Vishṇu	South side of great mound. (Nos. 5-7, said to have been "carefully fixed inside the temple.")	Ditto 68
8	Three fragments of the sculptured canopy and frame of a small statue; containing a miniature representation of the Dying Buddha, 2½ inches long, and having remains of an inscription on the back, including the name *Sāriputrasya.*	South side of temple ...	Ditto 68, 69, and XXII, Plate IV.
9	Seated Buddha, a foot high, with Buddhist creed in mediæval characters on back.	Inside a small votive *stūpa* to south.	Ditto XVIII, 69, and XXII, Plate IV.
10	Female figure in dark-coloured stone ...	Inside votive *stūpa* close to No. 9.	Ditto, XVIII, 70.

[1] During the passage of this paper through the press, this slab has been found at the Collector's house, where it was removed for safe custody. It will be sent to the Lucknow Provincial Museum. The inscription is very imperfect, and the date has been lost. It gives a long genealogy of a line of kings, including near the end Lakshmana, Māja Dēvi and Çivu Māja. The record is in characters of the eleventh or twelfth century.

Number.	Object.	Where found.	Reference.
11	Small copper-plate, about 4½" × 1," inscribed with Buddhist creed in characters supposed by Carlleyle to be of 5th century. I should refer the characters rather to the 8th or 9th century.	In deep excavation in front of temple of Dying Buddha.	*Reports*, XVIII, 70, and XXII, Plate IV.
12	Twenty terracotta seals, or votive tablets, with Buddhist creed in characters of later date.	At back of temple ...	Ditto, XVIII, 70
13	Ornamentally carved huge bricks, with beautiful devices.	In core of great *stúpa* ...	Ditto, 74
14	Terracotta seals or votive tablets ...	In Rámabhár *stúpa* (during Mr. Lamsden's excavation).	Ditto, 75
15	Ash and charcoal	In barrows	Ditto, 94
16	Two pots of cowries ...	In temple adjoining seated statue of Máthá Kúar.	Not mentioned by Carlleyle. The *gorait* said he saw them found.

This list proves that inscriptions exist in the ruins, and raises reasonable hopes that some record may be found which will definitely determine the identification of the spot.

I think that it would be worth while to undertake excavations. If the Kôṭ is proved to be the Charcoal Tope, or any other place visited by the Chinese pilgrims, the determination will be most valuable, and will go a long way towards settling the positions of Kapilavastu, Kuçanagara, and all the intermediate stages.

At present no point on the pilgrims' route between Çrâvastî and Vaiśâli has been determined.

All the identifications made by Cunningham and Carlleyle, which all depend on erroneous identifications of Kapilavastu and Kuçanagara, are demonstrably wrong.

11th *July*, 1896. V. A. SMITH.